First Year Letters

P9-BAT-988

Mrs. Hartwell
ROOM 203
BINJET SCHOOL

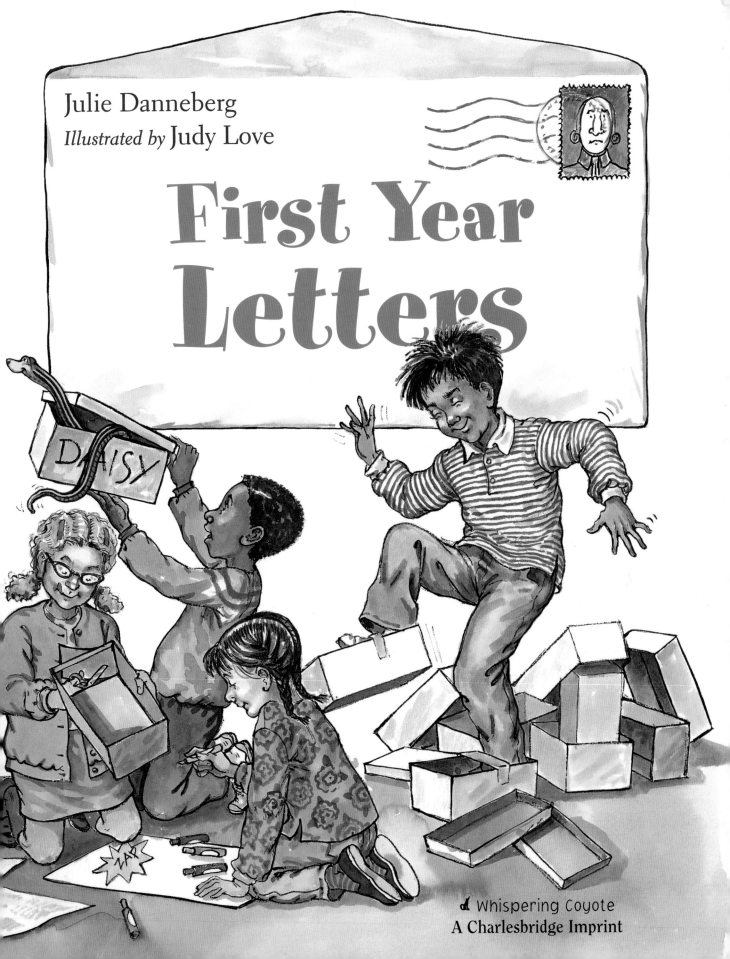

To Walker, with my love and thanks
—J. D.

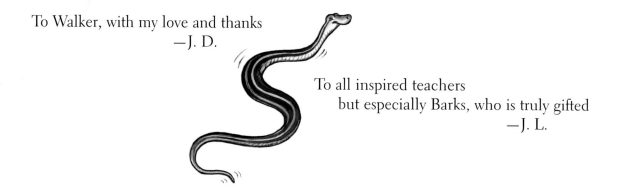

To all inspired teachers
but especially Barks, who is truly gifted
—J. L.

A Whispering Coyote Book
Text copyright © 2003 by Julie Danneberg
Illustrations copyright © 2003 by Judy Love
All rights reserved, including the right of reproduction in whole or in
part in any form. Charlesbridge, Whispering Coyote, and colophon
are registered trademarks of Charlesbridge Publishing, Inc.

Published by Charlesbridge
85 Main Street
Watertown, MA 02472
(617) 926-0329
www.charlesbridge.com

Library of Congress Cataloging-in-Publication Data
Danneberg, Julie, 1958–
    First Year Letters/ Julie Danneberg; illustrated by Judy Love.
        p. cm.
    "A Whispering Coyote book."
    Summary: The children in Mrs. Sarah Jane Hartwell's class write
her letters.
    ISBN 1-58089-084-9 (reinforced for library use)
    ISBN 1-58089-085-7 (softcover)
    [1. Teachers—Fiction. 2. Schools—Fiction. 3. Letters—Fiction.]
    I. Love, Judith DuFour, ill. II. Title.
    PZ7.D2327 Fl 2003
    [E]—dc21   2002002286

Printed in China
(hc) 10 9 8 7 6 5 4 3
(sc) 10 9 8 7 6 5 4

Illustrations in this book done in transparent dyes on Strathmore paper
Display type and text type set in Spumoni and Electra
Color separations by Regent Publishing Services
Printed and bound by Regent Publishing Services
Production supervision by Brian G. Walker
Designed by Diane M. Earley

September 9

Dear Mrs. Hartwell,

On the first day of school, I thought I saw your hand shake when you wrote your name on the chalkboard. That's when I figured you might be a little scared, just like me. And that made me feel better. Then you asked me to help you set up our brand-new classroom post office. And that's when I figured this is going to be a great year!

Thanks,
Shannon

October 14

Dear Mrs. Hartwell,

I thought of a few more things to add to our list of Important Things Teachers Should Know.
1. On pizza day we cannot be late. The pepperoni pieces go fast.
2. More recess, please.
3. Bringing Friday treats is a great idea, but just so you know, most kids don't eat broccoli or cauliflower unless they have to.

From,
Andy

P.S. Can this letter count as my example of a friendly letter?

Dear Mrs. Hartwell,

November 8

When Mrs. Burton came into our class today, your face turned really red. I peeked to see what she was writing. I couldn't read a word! Did you know Mrs. Burton has very messy handwriting?

Sincerely,
Carl

November 19

Dear Mrs. Hartwell,

Thank you for the delicious chocolate chip cookies. I'm sure Eddie didn't barf because of your baking! Actually, I think he got sick because he is a big, fat cookie hog!

After you left to clean your shoes, Gordon, the janitor, said you'd probably never come back. I'm really glad you did.

Very sincerely,
Maria

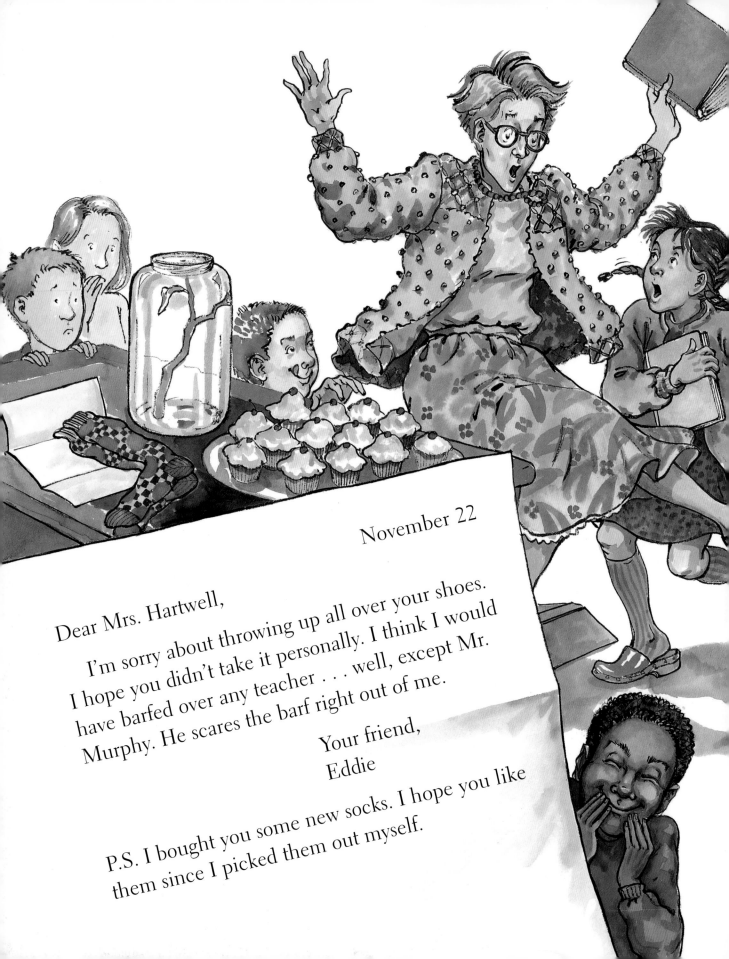

November 22

Dear Mrs. Hartwell,

I'm sorry about throwing up all over your shoes. I hope you didn't take it personally. I think I would have barfed over any teacher . . . well, except Mr. Murphy. He scares the barf right out of me.

Your friend,
Eddie

P.S. I bought you some new socks. I hope you like them since I picked them out myself.

Dear Mrs. Hartwell,

December 3

Mrs. Burton is making me write this letter during detention. I'm supposed to tell you sorry for ruining our reading party. I'm not quite sure how Daisy got loose. While you were chasing her down the hall, Mrs. Burton came in and told us to get started on our math. The day went downhill after that.

Sincerely,
Andy

P.S. I'm sure Daisy will come back soon.

December 10

Dear Mrs. Hartwell,

Thanks to you, science is my all-time favorite subject!
I thought Firefighter Phil was nice, didn't you? I think
I'll write him a letter!

Scientifically yours,
Jack

P.S. When you wear your safety goggles, you look just
like my frog, Benny.

December 14

Dear Mrs. Hartwell,

I sure enjoyed our field trip to the museum. That guard almost had a heart attack! You jumped over the railing like a real track star! Good thing too, because if that buffalo had fallen over, all those cute little prairie dogs would have been smashed to smithereens.

Excitedly yours,
Margaret

IN THIS CLASSROOM
EVERYONE IS A STUDENT
EVERYONE IS A TEACHER

January 5

Dear Mrs. Hartwell,

I liked our discussion about good students and good teachers during circle time yesterday. I also liked the sign we made for our door.

Sincerely,
Alexandra

P.S. I made a sign just like that and put it up in my kitchen at home. My mom told me to do a little less teaching and a little more learning. You need to explain things to her.

February 3

Dear Mrs. Hartwell,
    Yesterday was THE BEST! You looked good except that your legs were too skinny and you needed more stuffing around the middle. I saw the other kids watching us when we went outside to look for your shadow. I bet they were jealous.

Sincerely,
Zack

March 25

Dear Mrs. Hartwell,

I really don't think I needed to hold your hand the whole time we were at the aquarium yesterday. On the bus ride back to school, Sam said that you were my girlfriend.

Sincerely,
Eddie

April 18

Dear Mrs. Hartwell,

I have enjoyed getting to know you and your class this year, but I must ask that from now on you refrain from using anything that burns, smokes, or even gets hot. By the way, tell everyone that I hung up all of their "thank you" letters at the firehouse.

Sincerely,
Phil

Dear Mrs. Hartwell,

May 27

You didn't look scared or nervous today when Mrs. Burton visited our class. I told her that you were my absolute favorite teacher, and guess what? She said that this school has never, ever, had a teacher quite like you. We sure are lucky!

Sincerely,
Carl

May 31

Dear Sarah Jane,

Please come to my office tomorrow at 3:00.

Mrs. Burton